THE LIVES OF GREAT ARTISTS

THE LIFE AND ART OF SALVADOR DALÍ

THE LIVES OF GREAT ARTISTS

THE LIFE AND ART OF SALVADOR DALÍ

CATHERINE INGRAM

ROSEN PUBLISHING
New York

This edition published in 2017 by

The Rosen Publishing Group, Inc.

29 East 21st Street

New York, NY 10010

Library of Congress Cataloging-in-Publication Data

Names: Ingram, Catherine, author. | Rae, Andrew (Illustrator), illustrator.

Title: The life and art of Salvador Dalí / Catherine Ingram.

Description: New York : Rosen Publishing, 2016. | Series: The lives of great artists | Includes bibliographical references and index.

Identifiers: LCCN 2016039090 | ISBN 9781499465808 (library bound)

Subjects: LCSH: Dalí, Salvador, 1904-1989—Juvenile literature. | Artists—Spain—Biography—Juvenile literature.

Classification: LCC N7113.D3 I54 2016 | DDC 709.2 [B] —dc23

LC record available at https://lccn.loc.gov/2016039090

Manufactured in the United States of America

Series editor: Catherine Ingram

This book was produced and published in 2014 by Laurence King Publishing Ltd., London.

Acknowledgments

For Matthew, with love.

A heartfelt thanks to Laurence King for taking on this nutty project, and I am extremely grateful to Angus Hyland for his creative direction. I would like to thank Jo Lightfoot for her continual support, Melissa Danny for her thoughtful direction and careful editing, and Julia Ruxton for sourcing such great images. Thanks to Jason Ribeiro for all his work on the design, and Melanie Mues for her creative contribution. A big thanks to Andrew Rae, who backed the project from the beginning. I am also very grateful to Sara Roveta for her encouragement and support in the early stages of the project, and Jo Marsh for all her generous suggestions.

I would like to thank my mum and dad for their support over the years. Thanks Lulu and Sam for all the fun times.

Catherine Ingram, 2013

About the Author

Catherine Ingram is a freelance art historian. She obtained a First Class Honours degree at Glasgow University, where she was a Honeyman scholar. After an MA in 19th-century art at the Courtauld Institute of Art, Catherine became a graduate scholar at Trinity College, Oxford. After finishing her D.Phil, she was made a Prize Fellow at Magdalen College, Oxford. Catherine has taught on the MA course at Christie's and lectured at Imperial College, teaching art history to undergraduate scientists. She has also run courses at the Tate Gallery and was a personal assistant at South London Gallery. She lives with her family in London.

About the Illustrator

Andrew Rae is an illustrator and member of the illustration collective Peepshow. He studied at Brighton University and has worked for many clients worldwide in advertising, print, publishing and animation. He currently lives and works in London.

Contents

Dalí with the painter Georges Mathieu and a 40-foot-long (12-meter) baguette, which they presented at the Foire de Paris
May 13, 1958

Salvador Dalí is one of the most popular artists in the world, known for his lavish lifestyle, his gravity-defying moustache and his bizarre art. Mimicking coffin bearers, Dalí and a team of bakers carry an almost 40-foot (12-meter) baguette across their shoulders. Leading the march, Dalí is solemn, but behind him one of the bakers smirks. The scene is funny: a super-sized baguette, an über-serious artist, and a giant crutch. This is the essence of Dalí's surrealism, where the ordinary becomes extraordinary.

Dalí saw himself as Renaissance master – a grand oil painter – yet he explodes out of the tidy discipline of fine art. People are captivated by the man. Photographer George Brassaï "liked his comic humour, always a step ahead of his ideas, liked his complexes, his seriousness, his wild imagination, liked the way his brain worked … [and] sometimes liked his paintings as well."

Dalí's commercial projects would open up the realm of art, but at the time he was scorned by the art world. Dalí did not care. He loved money, and the Dalí phenomenon made millions. His megalomania knew no bounds. "Every morning upon awakening, I experience a supreme pleasure: that of being Salvador Dalí, and I ask myself, wonderstruck, what prodigious thing will he do today, this Salvador Dalí."

Family Life

Salvador Dalí Domènech was born on May 11, 1904 to Felipa Domènech Ferrés and Salvador Dalí Cusí. He had a younger sister, Ana María. His elder brother, after whom Dalí was named, died of gastroenteritis just before his second birthday. Salvador Cusí was a successful lawyer and the family lived well. For the first ten years of Dalí's life they lived at 6 Carrer Monturiol, Figueres, in northeastern Spain. According to Dalí, he was the king of his household: "I was allowed to do anything I pleased. I was the absolute monarch of the house. Nothing was good enough for me. My mother and father worshipped me." Dalí was adored and his every whim indulged. When he woke, his mother would ask him: "Sweetheart, what do you wish? Sweetheart, what do you want?"

Schoolboy Memories

When Dalí turned four, his father sent him to the state primary school. Most of the children were poor and Dalí, dressed like a little prince, stuck out and was bullied. He was probably very unhappy, but later, in his autobiography *The Secret Life of Salvador Dalí*, he views his isolation and loneliness as a sign of his own superiority. His first teacher, Esteban Trayter, was a "phantastic character," with crystal blue eyes, and a beard that hung in two symmetrical plaits to his knees. He ransacked old churches and brought his treasures into school to show his class. Dalí was fascinated by Trayter's art collection, especially a picture of a Russian girl swathed in furs, which he believed was an image of his future wife, Gala.

After two years Dalí's schoolwork had deteriorated: he had forgotten the alphabet, which his mother had taught him at home. His father was outraged and moved him to a French-speaking school that stood on a wasteland on the outskirts of Figueres. With all lessons in French, Dalí was left even more confused. He spent his time there daydreaming, staring out of the classroom window at the cypress trees, which appeared "dark red as though … dipped in wine." At home he daydreamed more. For hours he would lie on his bed gazing at moisture stains on his bedroom ceiling, imagining the brown blots as figures.

Storymakers

Dalí came from a family of storymakers, who embellished their past to impress. Dalí's father told everyone that his own father had been a doctor, but he had actually traded as a corkmaker. When Dalí's grandfather committed suicide by jumping from a building, the family's story was that he had died tragically of a brain trauma. Following family tradition, Dalí creates his mythology: in his autobiography *Secret Life* he reinvents his childhood, giving it the colour, intrigue and darkness appropriate for a genius painter.

AT THE AGE OF SIX I WANTED TO BE A COOK.
AT SEVEN I WANTED TO BE NAPOLEON.
FINALLY HE SETTLED THAT...
I'LL BE A GENIUS, AND THE WORLD WILL ADMIRE ME.

Power Hungry

Dalí was haunted by his brother's memory. He was the second Salvador. When he was a boy, his parents took him to his brother's grave and told him that he was the reincarnation of his brother. He grew up in his brother's shadow, as he tells: "My brother and I resembled each other like two drops of water, but we had different reflections. Like myself he had the unmistakable facial morphology of a genius. He gave signs of alarming precocity, but his glance was veiled by the melancholy characterizing insurmountable intelligence. I, on the other hand, was much less intelligent, but I reflected everything."

Dalí became obsessed with power. In his *Secret Life* he describes (or perhaps invents) incidents from his childhood that reflect his forcefulness, even cruelty: he tells of kicking his sister, and throwing a child off a bridge. His ruthless ambition grew, and he continued his tyranny into old age, when he carried a set of bells that he would regularly ring – "How else would I be sure that they would notice me?"

As a child, Dalí felt entitled to everything. His sister recounts: "Receiving presents was to prove one of Dalí's lifelong addictions. He usually abstained from giving them." On the rare occasions that a whim could not be satisfied he would fly into a rage, like the day he saw a string of candy hanging in a shop window, but the shop was closed so it couldn't possibly be bought. Dalí was livid, and inconsolable. Felipa's approach was always to appease her son, rather than challenge him. The Child King learnt to rule, and conquer.

Quiet Moments

There were peaceful times in the Dalí home. Salvador Cusí was interested in music, and collected La Sardana folk tunes. He would organize soirees with his neighbours. The children were allowed to stay up, and they would all dance. The Dalís enjoyed long holidays by the coast on the Cap de Creus peninsula. On their first trips they stayed with family friends, and later they bought a house on the beach near Cadaqués. Dalí was very happy there; at school he writes: "Throughout these days I have thought of nothing but Cadaqués. Every day I joyfully study my calendar and see how many days are left." Through his life Dalí lived in many different cities around the world, but the Cap de Creus remained his haven; as he reflects: "I am home only here. Elsewhere, I am camping out."

THE PYRENEES
THE TORTOISE ROCK
THE CAMEL ROCK
DARNIUS
AFTER HIS FATHER BANISHED HIM FROM CADAQUÉS, DALÍ SETTLED WITH HIS WIFE, GALA, AT PORT LLIGAT.
PORT LLIGAT
DALÍ'S HOME
CADAQUÉS
THE DALÍS HOLIDAY HOME
ES LLANER BEACH
SMUGGLERS HID THEIR TREASURE IN LOCAL COVES.
GALA'S CASTLE
PÚBOL
THE OLIVE TREES WERE GROWN IN ROWS, ENCLOSED IN DRY SLATE WALLS.
ES SORTELL BEACH
CALA NANS LIGHTHOUSE

CADAQUÉS AND THE CAP DE CREUS PENINSULA

THE DALÍS HAD A HOLIDAY HOME IN CADAQUÉS. THE HOUSE BACKED STRAIGHT ONTO THE BEACH, WHERE THE YOUNG DALÍ WOULD WANDER FOR HOURS ON END. DALÍ FELT A DEEP CONNECTION WITH THE DRAMATIC LANDSCAPE OF THE CAP DE CREUS PENINSULA: ITS RAW, RED EARTH, COARSE VEGETATION, AND THE GREAT ROCKS WITH THEIR ANTHROPOMORPHIC FORMS. DALÍ MET GALA, HIS FUTURE WIFE, ON THE BEACH OF CADAQUÉS. IN 1929 HE WAS BANISHED FROM THE VILLAGE BY HIS FATHER. DALÍ AND GALA MOVED A SHORT DISTANCE UP THE COAST TO PORT LLIGAT AND SPENT OVER 50 YEARS REDESIGNING FIVE HUMBLE FISHERMEN'S COTTAGES INTO AN AMAZING SURREAL RESIDENCE. IN 1969 DALÍ BOUGHT GALA HER OWN CASTLE AT PÚBOL.

A Morphing Reality

Eroded by the Tramontana wind and seawater into spectacular organic and anthropomorphic forms, the Great Rocks off the coast of Cadaqués were part of local folklore, and Dalí came to "know by heart each contour of the rocks." They provided him with a "visual dictionary"; he reproduced their textured surfaces and spectacular shapes in his paintings. For Dalí, their outstanding feature was the way they appeared to metamorphose into new forms, as he describes: "As we moved forward with the characteristic slowness of a row-boat ... all these images became transfigured ... the tips of the anvil had become rounded, and it was exactly like a woman ... " Later Dalí would explore different ways of showing things morphing in his paintings and films.

The Comfort of Strangers

In Dalí's time, there were no good roads to Cadaqués. Isolated, the village had a stark charm. The unadorned, white buildings stacked up like children's building bricks, and fish bones were used to pave the streets. Everyday life was primitive: water had to be collected from a well and, since the electricity rarely worked, the houses were lit by candlelight. Left to his own devices Dalí was at the mercy of strangers. The fishermen were kind to him, and would row him around the Great Rocks. Dalí befriended the village smuggler (who let him use his hut as a studio) and the "local witch," Lidia Nogueres. Later, in his *Secret Life*, Dalí glorifies Lidia's savage behaviour: "[she] sat on the floor ... she adroitly plunged her scissors into the chicken's neck and held its bleeding head in a deep glazed terracotta vessel." According to Dalí, he later based his "paranoiac-critical method" on Lidia's paranoid state of mind. The relationships formed at Cadaqués set up a lifelong pattern. Dalí was drawn to intense characters, as friend Carlos Lozano later recognized: "The overtly normal infuriated Dalí." The Child King wanted to be entertained. According to him: "You are here to give and receive pleasure. You must tell me things that are interesting. I am in a state of permanent intellectual [excitement] ... Cultivate a story as you would a plant, nurse it, and nurture it."

The Washroom Studio

In July 1912 the family moved to a different apartment on Carrer Monturiol. This apartment had a rooftop terrace; the Child King relished the high vantage point, as he tells: "The whole panorama, as far as the Bay of Roses, seemed to obey me and depend upon my glance ...." Dalí convinced his mother to let him use an old laundry room on the roof as an art room. His studio was tiny, but Dalí was enterprising. He sat in the cement basin to paint; in the summer months, when it got very hot, he would run water up to his waist. He also turned the old washboard into an easel, and painted on hatboxes from his aunt's millinery shop.

A Visual Mind

In his studio Dalí stored his collection of Gowan's art books, which his father picked up for him. The series was unusual: with hardly any text, each volume provided a visual history of one of the Great Masters in 60 black-and-white illustrations. The pictures were so vivid to Dalí that they seemed real. Later Dalí remembers the Ingres volume, and "falling in love" with the naked girl in *The Fountain*. He talks as if he inhabited the pictures. Reflecting on the series another time, he says: "I feel sure that I have picnicked once in that shady Watteau glade or that [I walked] through one of those landscapes used by Titian."

Dalí grew up during a visual revolution, which saw the birth of cinema and photojournalism. He was fascinated by the new technology. His first teacher, Esteban Trayter, had a collection of stereoscopic viewers, and he let Dalí and the other boys use them. Dalí was intrigued by the viewers, which gave images an eerie three-dimensional quality.

The first cinema in Figueres had opened in the year of Dalí's birth, and as a treat he was taken to see the new releases on a Saturday morning. According to many historians, at the first cinema viewings people often panicked and screamed. The films often didn't have a story. With roots in turn-of-the-century fairground spectacles, they ran visual "gags" that played on the uncanny, and ultimately aimed to shock the spectator. Filmmakers would start with a "still" picture that would then be transformed in some way – for example, a stationary train would come to life and rush at the viewer, belching smoke.

Like so many, Dalí was captivated. His mother bought a hand-held projector, and she would project short films onto the wall at home. The language of early cinema is very relevant to Dalí. He liked to shock his audience, and was very interested in showing things in the process of transformation. Dalí kept up to date with the development of cinema and photography, and replicated cinematic effects in his art.

Precocious Talent

Dalí showed artistic talent from an early age. In June 1916, when only 12 years old, he went to stay with family friends, the Pichots. It turned into an experiment in Impressionism. The Pichot estate – with its wheat fields and olive groves – looked like an Impressionist scene, and Ramon Pichot, a successful Impressionist painter, introduced Dalí to Impressionist techniques. Struck by the radical use of colour and the raw brushwork, Dalí wrote, "I did not have eyes enough to see all that I wanted in those thick and formless daubs of paint... [it] burned deep in my throat like a drop of Armagnac swallowed the wrong way." Playing magician, he walked around the grounds looking into a crystal decanter stopper, which created the fragmented illusion of Impressionist art. After his visit to the Pichots, Dalí painted *View of Cadaqués with Shadow of Mount Pani*. It is a typical Impressionist painting: signature coloured strokes of paint record light effects. However, Impressionism was a short-lived experiment. Dalí did not identify with the pastoral agricultural scenes; he preferred the drama and magic of the Cadaqués landscape.

Ramon Pichot advised Dalí's father to enrol him in the Municipal Drawing School in Figueres. The art teacher, Juan Núñez, recognized Dalí's talent and helped him to develop his techniques. Dalí credits Núñez as being the most important mentor in his development as an artist. At the end of his first year, Dalí was awarded a certificate of excellence, and in his honour his father held a little exhibition at their apartment in Figueres.

The Academy of San Fernando, Madrid, 1922–26

In 1921 Dalí's mother died of uterine cancer. According to Dalí, his loss made him even more determined to succeed: "I swore ... [to] snatch my mother from death and destiny with the swords of light that some day would savagely gleam around my glorious name." The following year, Dalí left home to study at the San Fernando Academy in Madrid. Art school was a disappointment to Dalí, who "immediately understood that those old professors covered in honours and decorations could not teach me anything." His teachers were following French Impressionism, which Dalí had already left behind. The Child King spoke out: in 1923 he was suspended for questioning the merits of a new teacher, and three years later he was expelled for saying that his teachers were unfit to examine his work. Nevertheless, Madrid was overall a positive experience. Dalí was inspired by the art at the Prado, especially the Velázquez collection, but the real highlight was the social life at the "Resi" – the hall of residence.

S. DALI

Dalí's Metamorphosis

The Resi was run by Alberto Jiménez Fraud. Modelling the Oxford and Cambridge system, he created a stimulating college scene, with lectures from the great thinkers of the day like Albert Einstein, and the library stocked with the latest theory. Sigmund Freud's texts had just been translated into Spanish, and Dalí and his friends read and discussed them at length. Dalí's student copy of Freud's *The Interpretation of Dreams* has numerous underlinings and annotations. Later he said that the text "presented itself as one of the capital discoveries in my life." It would be a few years before Dalí explored Freudian ideas in his art.

Dalí found like-minded people at the Resi. He was part of an arty group that included filmmaker Luis Buñuel and poet Federico García Lorca. Relationships were not easy as there was a lot of jealousy and rivalry. Initially the Child King resented the group's leader: "I knew Lorca would shine like a mad and fiery diamond. Suddenly I would set off at a run, and no one would see me for three days."

Lorca and Dalí became infatuated with each other. In his poetry, Lorca celebrated "Salvador Dalí, with your olive-coloured voice," and Dalí painted Lorca as the divine figure of Saint Sebastian. Together they developed a theory on art. Art historian Mary Ann Caws argues that "some of Dalí's richest writings on his own painting are addressed to the poet." Dropping the hyperbole, Dalí talks intimately to Lorca. A warmer, poetical side to the artist emerges: "I feel a love of the grass, thorns in the palm of the hand, ears red against the sun." Lorca tried to seduce Dalí, but according to the artist, nothing much happened. His mother had been a devout Catholic and homosexuality was illegal – perhaps Dalí was fearful. Their relationship more or less ended when Dalí met his future wife. Dalí was always guarded about his sexual identity.

Dalí's new friends were all dandies, known for their luxurious lifestyle and smart dressing. When Dalí arrived at art school, he played the part of the romantic artist. He dressed head-to-toe in black, whitened his skin, dyed his hair black, and used black kohl round his eyes. But the Child King saw the potential of the dandy image and so he decided: "Tomorrow I am going to dress like everyone else." Dalí thought that if he behaved like royalty, he would be treated like royalty. It seemed to work. On a student income, he feasted at Madrid's grandest hotels, and his lavish lifestyle was paid for by friends, family, and art collectors. Dalí's love of money, and fame, would come to annoy the art world.

IN HIS "SECRET LIFE," DALÍ DESCRIBES THE DAY OF TRANSFORMATION:
... HE VISITED A BARBER, WHO CUT OFF HIS LONG HAIR ...
... HE SELECTED AN EXPENSIVE TWEED SUIT ...
... HE BOUGHT A BLUE SILK SHIRT ...
... THE FINEST SAPPHIRE CUFFLINKS ...
... AND A BAMBOO CANE.
LATER HE USED PAINT VARNISH TO HOLD HIS SLICK HAIRSTYLE ...
VARNISH
... AND WAXED HIS MOUSTACHE INTO ITS SIGNATURE TWIRL.

Dalí's Art, 1922–26

According to the poet José Moreno Villa, during his time at art school "Dalí plays two apparently opposing cards ... the 'traditional card' alongside the card of audacity." Dalí worked his way through the European avant-garde styles. After Impressionism he experimented with Neo-Impressionism, Futurism, and Cubism. At exhibition his displays were often criticized for being an odd assortment of miscellaneous styles.

A more singular vision emerges in a series of intimate portraits of his sister, Ana María. In *Figure at a Window*, Dalí shows his sister looking out at the seascape of Cadaqués. A harmony in grey and blue, the piece has a classical austerity. Every element is carefully balanced: the shoreline echoes the horizontal axis of the windowpane, while the vanishing point is marked out by the direction of the floorboards and the window slats.

Within this ordered universe lies an "obsessive realism." Dalí records every element with startling precision, from the hairs on his sister's head and the creases on her dress, to the house reflected in the windowpane. His attention to every detail creates a frozen, hyper-real effect. In 1926 Dalí started to look beyond the family, and returned to the Cadaqués landscape, representing it in the same hard-edged naturalism.

Picasso saw this portrait in Dalí's first one-man show at the Sala Dalmau, and he liked it very much. He recommended Dalí to his friends, the art dealers Paul Rosenberg and Pierre Loeb, and Loeb took a trip to Spain with the sole purpose of viewing Dalí's recent work. Loeb did not offer anything, but Picasso would remain a loyal supporter. When Dalí moved to Paris, Picasso tried to help him again, this time introducing him to his patron, Gertrude Stein, although nothing came from this meeting either. In time Picasso would become more circumspect, and distance himself from the flamboyant Surrealist artist.

Figure at a Window
Salvador Dalí, 1925

Oil on cardboard (masonite)
41¼ × 29¼ in (105 × 74.5 cm)
Museo Nacional Centro de Arte Reina Sofía, Madrid

Penya-Segats (Woman on the Rocks)
Salvador Dalí, 1926

Oil on olive wood panel
10¼ × 15¾ in (26 × 40 cm)
Private collection

The Extraordinary in the Ordinary

In the mid-1920s Dalí started writing about art. His essays develop ideas that he discussed with Lorca. He rejected the tendency in art to beautify and idealize, and condemned expressive art; he and Lorca used the derogatory term "putrefact" to describe art concerned with feelings and emotion. After excluding emotion, and beauty, Dalí set the parameters for a crisp, objective art. In a letter home, Dalí writes, "I'm inventing a new way which is purely natural ... that captures ... the outside of things." His attention to detail was appreciated by a Cadaqués fisherman who praised Dalí's rendering of the sea, "because one can count the waves." Dalí even celebrated this underlying obsessiveness in a work called *Poem of Little Things*, where he repeats the words "little things" twelve times in succession.

Penya-Segats (Woman on the Rocks) is a geological masterpiece. The texture and materiality of everything is conveyed: the rocks appear hard, sharp, and crystalline, and the cliffs seem to melt into the sea abruptly, just as Dalí describes the headland of the Cap de Creus, "the spot where the Pyrenees come down into the sea in a grandiose, geological delirium."

Dalí's naturalism is somehow haunting. While normal perception is graded, Dalí's "extended" gaze flattens the depth of field. He observes the world with, as he says, "the anaesthetized look of the clearest eye, without eyelashes." In this painting, like in the portrait of his sister, his detailed transcription is extraordinary. With every "little thing" in sharp focus, we see the world intensified. Undulating patterns loom from the rock surface. This painting unlocks a "marvellous" beauty in Cadaqués.

The Naked Lady

But what about the naked lady? The pale, white nude seems so out of place by the craggy cliffs of Cadaqués. A classical figure, she belongs in a Claude Lorrain painting or Titian's pastoral landscape. It is worth remembering that as a boy, Dalí pored over his Gowan's art series, and imagined himself picnicking with such fictional characters. To him, they were as real as the Great Rocks of Cadaqués.

Dalí in Paris

In April 1926 Dalí travelled to Paris – the epicentre of art. He explored the Louvre and studied the Great Masters. The avant-garde scene thrilled him. He visited Picasso, who showed him his art and talked to the young artist about his own work. Between 1926 and 1927 Dalí explored a Cubist language, painting Cubist subjects (still lifes and portraits) and rendering in flat, Cubist planes.

Dalí also met up with a number of Surrealists, including the leader of the movement, André Breton. Through the years Dalí had a tumultuous relationship with the Surrealists, but there were important overlaps in their thinking. Like Dalí, the Surrealists were interested in the "extra-ordinary": Breton sought a "marvellous beauty." Dalí was impressed by the "intensity" of Surrealist paintings: the dream landscapes of Max Ernst and Yves Tanguy, and Giorgio de Chirico's atmospheric paintings, with their looming shadows, open portals, and elongated perspectives.

Giorgio de Chirico
Melancholy and Mystery of a Street, 1914.
Oil on canvas. 34¼ × 28⅛ in (87.1 × 71.4 cm).
Private Collection

Dabbling with Surrealism, 1927–28

Between 1927 and 1928, Dalí kept his distance from the Surrealists. In these early days the Surrealists focused on the involuntary stream of unconscious thinking. In their first Manifesto, published in 1924, André Breton defined Surrealism as: "Pure psychic automatism, by which one proposes to express, either verbally, in writing, or by any other manner, the real functioning of thought. Dictation of thought in the absence of all control exercised by reason, outside of all aesthetic and moral preoccupation."

The Surrealists developed the technique of "automatic" drawing, which involved the artist allowing his pen to wander, and unconscious processes to unfold. André Masson's *Automatic Drawing* is a typical example – a mesh of lines record the stream of the unconscious, and a few, indistinct images loom out of the chaotic scribbles. Dalí briefly experimented with the method, but he quickly rejected it, along with the Surrealists' focus on "murky subconscious processes." He was interested in the idea of surreality, but thought it could be found in "pure, crystalline objectivity."

André Masson
Automatic Drawing, 1924.
Ink on paper. 9¼ × 8⅛ in (23.5 × 20.6 cm). Museum of Modern Art, New York. Given anonymously (873.1978)

Photography

From the mid-1920s Dalí heralded the "clear objectivity of the little camera." For Dalí, the advantage of celluloid was that it left a direct imprint of reality, and conveyed things with startling "precision." Dalí was sensitive to the language of photography and film, and replicated technical effects in his art. In *Futile Efforts* he uses the camera close up: the human body is revealed in microscopic detail – the torso bares unsightly folds, and the skin bristles with wiry hairs.

In his essay, "Photography, Pure Creation of the Mind," Dalí points to the poetry of photography and, indeed, how it answers Breton's call for the marvellous in art. He describes how the "close-up" and "a simple change of scale [cause] unusual similarities, and ... undreamt-of analogies." He illustrates another essay with a photograph of a marabou eye from a book by László Moholy-Nagy. The photo is incredible, with layers of coexisting worlds: the marabou's wrinkled skin is like a burrowed landscape, and reflected in the animal's dark pupil is the shadow of a man wearing a hat, and beyond him lies a cluster of trees.

Like the layered worlds reflected in the marabou eye, *Futile Efforts* is a "marvellous" juxtaposition of different realities, though far more sinister. The amalgam of fragmented torsos, decapitated heads, decomposing animals, and blood pools suggests a disturbed, paranoid psyche.

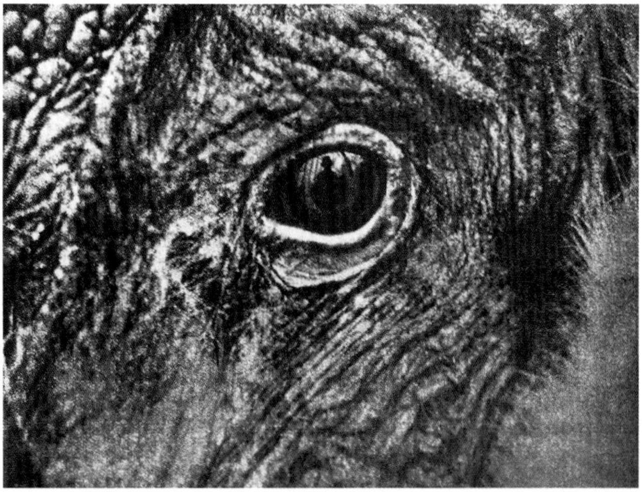

Eye of a Marabou
From *Painting, Photography & Film* (1925)
by László Moholy-Nagy

Honey Is Sweeter than Blood

While remaining wary of Surrealism, more and more Dalí borrowed from their repertoire. He started exploring a central theme of Surrealism: dreams. In his study for *Honey Is Sweeter than Blood* we enter a dream. Everything is asleep. The body is slumped in slumber, and the eyes of the severed head are closed. As the body rests, "the mind" – centre of imagination and dreams – is brightly coloured and full of life. Dream thoughts are presented in scattered images, such as the rotting donkey and swarming ants. Dalí attempts to show multiple states of being: the breasts in the sky also look like winking eyes. The analogy lacks the intensity of the marabou's eye.

The format is similar to the esoteric landscapes of Yves Tanguy, which Dalí had seen in Paris the year before. Like Tanguy, Dalí uses a sharp horizon line to separate the sky from the amorphous landscape, and a stock of strange biomorphic and geometric forms cast eerie shadows.

The aggressive energy sat uncomfortably with André Breton. Desperately wanting Dalí to join Surrealism, Breton politely tiptoed round the decapitated heads, the blood, and later excrement stains in Dalí's paintings. Meanwhile Dalí started pouring it out. In March 1929 he moved to Paris to work with his old college friend Luis Buñuel on their horrifying film: *Un Chien Andalou*.

Yves Tanguy
Mama, Papa Is Wounded!, 1927.
Oil on canvas. 36¼ × 28¾ in
(92.1 × 73 cm).
Museum of Modern Art, New York.
Purchase (78.1936)

Surreality in Film

Dalí and Buñuel took only a few months to create *Un Chien Andalou*. The film is haunting – ants crawl out of a hole in a man's hand, a rotting donkey lies stretched across a piano – but it is the first scene that really shocks. It opens with a man looking pensively across at a white moon. The whiteness of the moon becomes the white of the eye of a young woman and the man calmly slits her eye open. To create the effect, Dalí and Buñuel used fast montage. They first filmed a dead animal's eye being slit open, and fluid bursting forth, and then superimposed the shot onto the view of the man holding open the woman's eye. Even when you know the gag, the visceral horror still resonates. Worried how people would react, Buñuel turned up to the premieres with rocks in his pockets in case the audience turned violent.

A Surrealist Battleground: "Blood, [Excrement], and Putrefaction"

After shooting *Un Chien Andalou*, and for the next five years, Dalí would spend most of his time in Paris. He despised the city with its "auto-punitive architecture" and fast pace of life, but he recognized that he needed to be there in order to launch his career and establish himself within the European avant-garde. Immediately he was exposed to the current avant-garde debates, and found himself jostled between two factions within Surrealism – Breton's idealism and Georges Bataille's brute materialism. Breton and Bataille, who had battled for leadership of the Surrealist movement, now fought to represent Dalí.

It is fair to say that Bataille understood Dalí better than Breton did. Bataille did not need to tiptoe round "blood, [excrement], and putrefaction." He appreciated the "terrifying ugliness" of Dalí's work. There is a lot of overlap in their thinking: like Dalí, Bataille felt that modern life had lost contact with concrete reality, with a base materiality. With fellow thinkers, Bataille set up the magazine *Documents* and, while Bataille courted Dalí, there was a natural exchange of ideas between them. The magazine includes "scrutinizing photos" – a close-up on a toe complete with gnarled nail and wiry hairs, a saliva-filled mouth, a dead fly – images that Dalí would have appreciated. Throughout the magazine there is a preoccupation with eroticism, death, and decay, themes that are central to Dalí's next piece, *The First Days of Spring*.

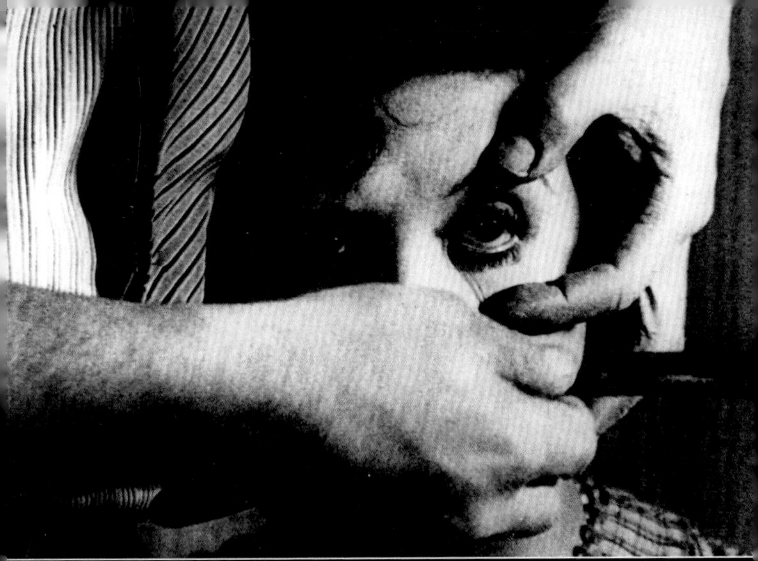

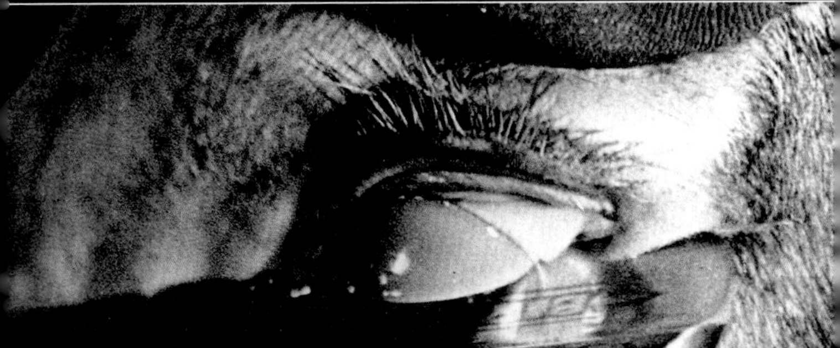

Film stills from *Un Chien Andalou*
Salvador Dalí and Luis Buñuel, 1929

The First Days of Spring
Salvador Dalí, 1929

Oil and collage on panel
19½ × 25½ in (49.5 × 64 cm)
Salvador Dalí Museum, St Petersburg, Florida
On loan from E. & A. Reynolds Morse

The First Days of Spring

Dalí's sister described *The First Days of Spring* as a "nightmare on canvas." We enter another dream world, but this time Freud's *Interpretation of Dreams* colours everything – indeed Freud himself appears in the picture as an old man dressed in a brown suit. Focused on Freud's idea that dreams can reveal painful childhood experiences, Dalí visualizes personal memories in brightly coloured symbols.

The giant locust attached to the sleeping head reflects Dalí's fear of insects. This phobia originated from an early childhood experience. In his *Secret Life* he recounts holding a vile and slimy slobberer fish, and being horrified to find that that the fish had the same face as a grasshopper. At school, bullies played on his fear and stuck grasshoppers down his shirt. By painting the locust's pincer over the disembodied mouth, and at the corner of the eye, he visualizes the awful sensation of insects crawling over his body. Alongside the fearful, there are also happy images from Dalí's past: the shape of the sleeping head has the form of one of the Great Rocks of Cadaqués. The animal imagery – the little deer and the eagle's head – are thought to be illustrations from his favourite books. The chubby pencil may be an image of his first crayon.

Dalí's evocation of dreams is sophisticated. He puts things together that do not belong with each other in everyday life, like the finger stuck onto the bucket. He shows how time and place become merged in dreams: Dalí appears as a baby (the photograph on the road), as a boy holding his father's hand (in the far distance), and as a man (in the foreground). He combines childhood fears with sexual desires. At the far left, a man fantasizes beside a naked woman.

Dalí shows things changing state, and grouped images are meant to be read as a sequence of morphing states. In the case of the cherub face that sits on the peculiar body form, we can decipher a few stages: the vein-like branch (a plant form) becomes a sleeping head and then a cherub's face. Actually, the projection does not really work, and Dalí was aware of it. *Un Chien Andalou* revealed to him that cinema was far more suited to showing transformation.

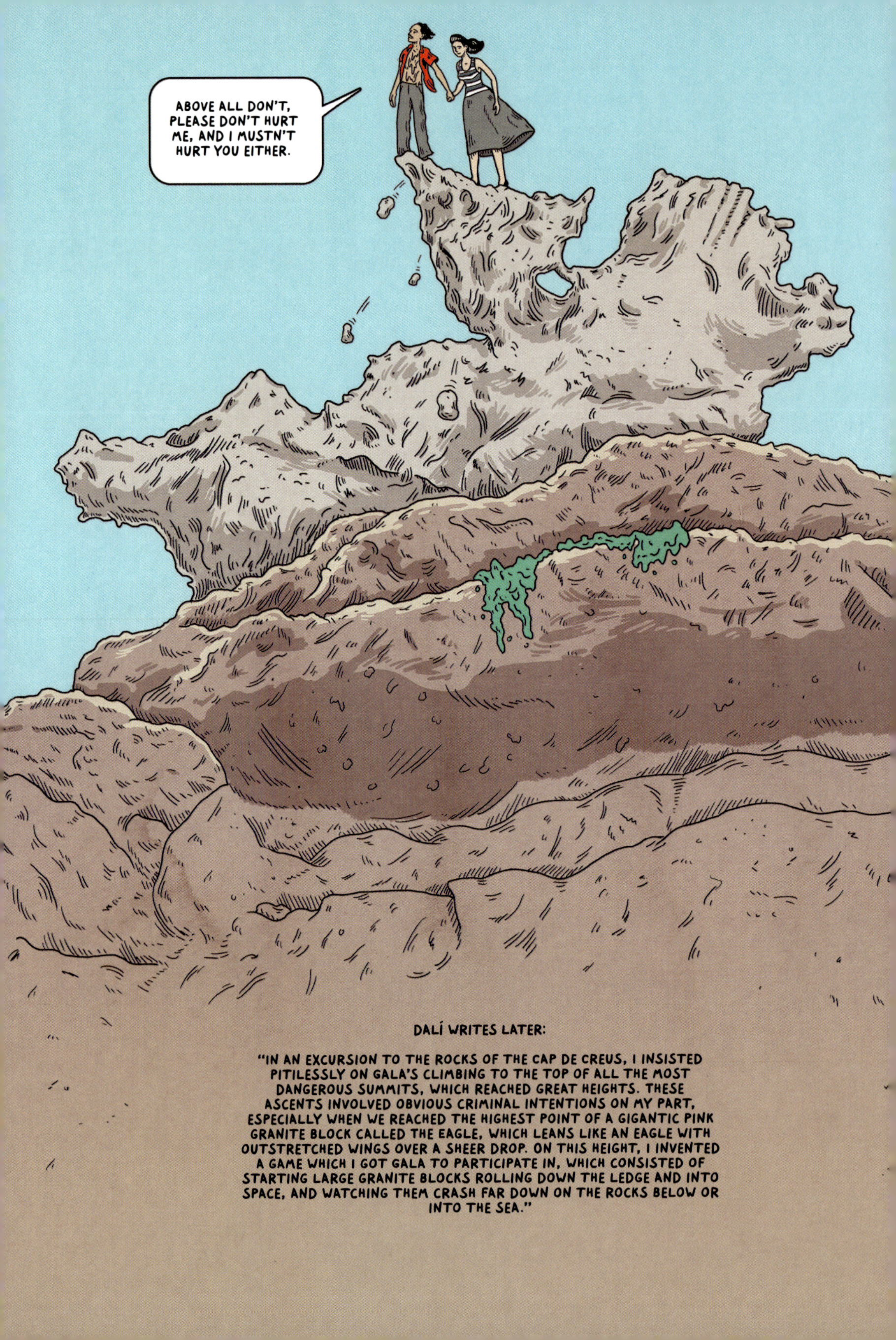
ABOVE ALL DON'T, PLEASE DON'T HURT ME, AND I MUSTN'T HURT YOU EITHER.
DALÍ WRITES LATER:
"IN AN EXCURSION TO THE ROCKS OF THE CAP DE CREUS, I INSISTED PITILESSLY ON GALA'S CLIMBING TO THE TOP OF ALL THE MOST DANGEROUS SUMMITS, WHICH REACHED GREAT HEIGHTS. THESE ASCENTS INVOLVED OBVIOUS CRIMINAL INTENTIONS ON MY PART, ESPECIALLY WHEN WE REACHED THE HIGHEST POINT OF A GIGANTIC PINK GRANITE BLOCK CALLED THE EAGLE, WHICH LEANS LIKE AN EAGLE WITH OUTSTRETCHED WINGS OVER A SHEER DROP. ON THIS HEIGHT, I INVENTED A GAME WHICH I GOT GALA TO PARTICIPATE IN, WHICH CONSISTED OF STARTING LARGE GRANITE BLOCKS ROLLING DOWN THE LEDGE AND INTO SPACE, AND WATCHING THEM CRASH FAR DOWN ON THE ROCKS BELOW OR INTO THE SEA."

The Child King Meets his Queen

Exhausted by work, Dalí retreated to the family home at Cadaqués. He was joined by the French poet Paul Eluard and his wife Gala. Dalí was immediately captivated by Gala, and Gala, as Dalí modestly recounts, "considered me a genius." Their courtship unfolded like a surreal drama: Dalí's initial choice of outfit for his first date was bizarre – a slashed silk shirt, a pair of trunks, and a string of pearls. He anointed himself with fish glue and goat manure, and stained his armpits with blood and blue paint. But before leaving he had a moment of doubt, had a quick wash and toned down his fashion. With the wild Tramontana wind blowing, he walked Gala across the Cap de Creus peninsula to show her the Eagle Rock.

Queen Gala

Later Dalí told society girl Amanda Lear, "I love to see Gala, all dressed up, bejewelled like a Queen." Shortly after their first meeting, Gala left her husband and her little girl to be with Dalí. Ten years older than Dalí, she took charge of him like a domineering mother. At their first meeting she told him, "My little boy, we shall never leave each other again." Infantilized, Dalí would go about his day without a penny in his pocket and Gala would scoop up the bills. Dalí was clearly happy to play along, as Lear remembers: "Whenever he received a cheque, he would immediately give it to Gala, who would put it straight into her handbag." Gala took control of the expanding Dalí empire, promoting his art and writing, securing art patrons, and organizing sales and exhibitions. Dalí often signed his work "Gala Salvador Dalí." People hated Gala's dominating ways. The art historian John Richardson wrote that most people "would agree that to know [Gala] was to loathe her." If Gala organized, Dalí reigned. Dalí describes sitting in his car, watching Gala change a tire in the pouring rain. Discussing the incident with Lear later, he admits, "Basically, I am a swine."

Joining Surrealism

In the summer of 1929 Dalí decided to join the Surrealist movement. Why at this point? He saw an opportunity and grabbed it. His plan was to "become leader as soon as possible." Breton probably thought Dalí's charisma would benefit the group and open up new parameters for Surrealist art. Including Dalí on his own terms, he celebrated the "hallucinatory" effect of Dalí's painting, arguing that Dalí transported the viewer to a mythical, ideal land. Their differences surfaced very quickly, but they did share an interest in Freudian theory. In 1938 Dalí visited Freud at his home in Elsworthy Road, London. Freud said very little as he had mouth cancer and talking was a struggle for him.

The First Days of Spring marked a change, and was Dalí's first rigorous attempt to visualize the unconscious in terms of Freudian theory. At that point he defined surrealism in Freudian terms. Arguing that Freud "revealed that the human body is full of secret drawers," Dalí celebrated the unconscious world as uncharted territory, where "surreal" things happened. In a number of later works, he depicts the human body as a cabinet or cupboard. In *The Anthropomorphic Cabinet* (this later sculpture is based on his 1936 painting) he opens the secret drawers of the unconscious and lets, as he says, "the countless narcissistic smells … waft out." The spindly veins, the worm-like hair, and the intestinal tubes falling out of the drawer are hideous. There is a sense of self-disgust, the feeling that Dalí's inner world is monstrous and repellent to others.

The Anthropomorphic Cabinet
Salvador Dalí, 1982
Conceived and first cast in 1982 from the paintings and drawings of 1936

Bronze with dark patina
23⅝ × 12½ in (60 × 31.7 cm)
Foundry Foneria Mibrosa, Barcelona, Private Collection

DALÍ'S CHEST OF DRAWERS

Dalí Disowned

1929 was an epic year for Dalí. He moved to Paris, fell in love, and joined the Surrealists. He started acting erratically, almost hysterically – as his first date with Gala reflects. Dalí's father was outraged by his son's behaviour, and his relationship with a married woman. Then he heard that Dalí had inscribed one of his paintings with: "Sometimes, for pleasure, I spit on my mother's portrait." Unsurprisingly, he took it as an insult to the memory of his late wife.

On December 6, 1929, Dalí received a letter from his father refusing to support him, and banishing him from Cadaqués. Versed in Freudian theory, he spoke about the psychological impact of his father's rejection, but took no responsibility for his own behaviour. Narcissistic to the core, Dalí almost relished the attention that arose from the unhappy event, and turned it into another drama. As a retort to his father, he cut off his hair and buried it on the beach at Cadaqués. He then shaved his scalp and asked Buñuel to photograph him with a sea urchin on his head.

Luis Buñuel
Dalí with sea urchin on his head, Cadaqués, 1929
Gelatin silver print, 11¾ × 7½ in (30 × 19 cm).
The Israel Museum. Gift of the Samuel Gorovoy Foundation, New York, to American friends of the Israel Museum (B89.0066)

Playing as King and Queen in Paris

The Parisian lifestyle was extremely stressful for Dalí and Gala. Poor as church mice, they lived among the rich and glamorous. Desperate to belong and impress, Dalí and Gala acted their parts. Like king and queen, they feasted with friends while Gala scampered round trying to sell his paintings and his new "surreal" wares. Dalí came up with some amazing designs; although Gala had no success selling them at the time, some of them have now become commercial products.

MIRRORED FINGERNAILS THAT LET YOU ADMIRE YOURSELF ON THE GO ...

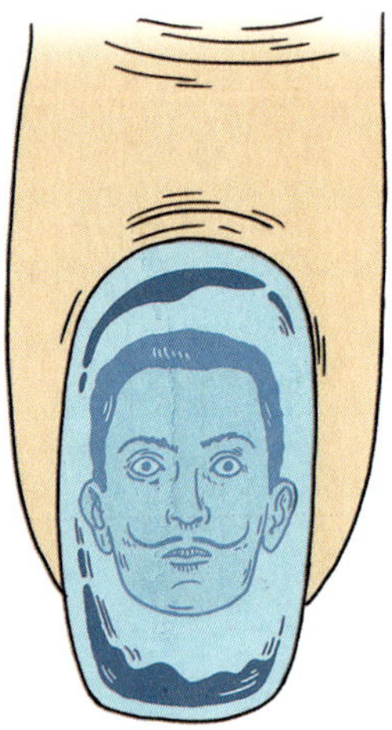

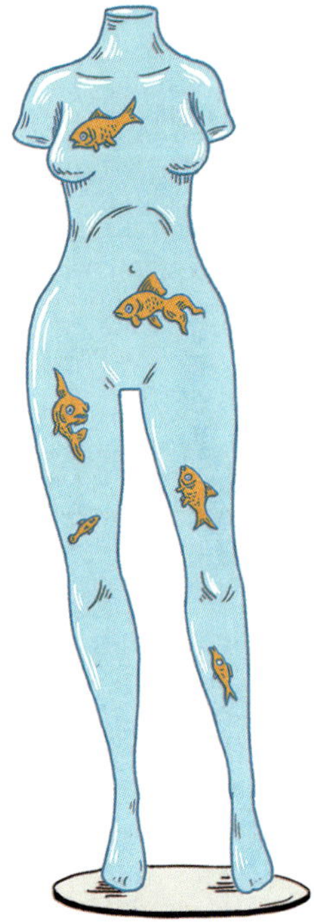

A SEE-THROUGH MANNEQUIN FILLED WITH WATER AND SWIMMING GOLDFISH ...

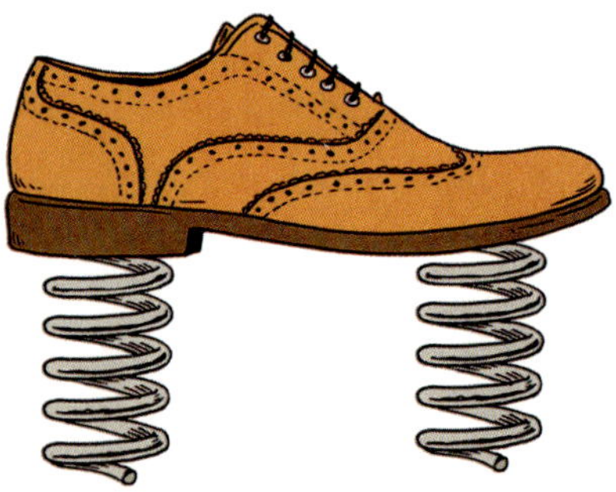

SHOES WITH SPRINGS ...

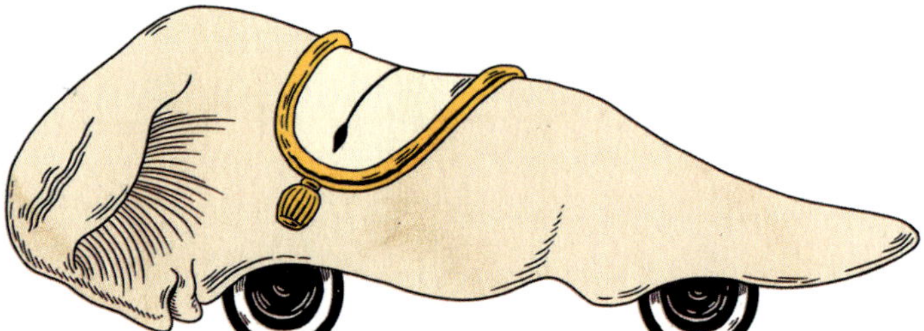

AN AERODYNAMIC CAR...

OFF WITH THE ROBES

IN 1929 GALA AND DALÍ BOUGHT A FISHERMAN'S COTTAGE IN THE VILLAGE OF PORT LLIGAT, NEAR CADAQUÉS. IT OFFERED A TRANQUIL REFUGE FROM THE PRESSURES OF CITY LIFE. THEIR TINY SHACK HAD NO ELECTRICITY OR RUNNING WATER. GALA AND DALÍ LOVED THE SOLITUDE AND THE SLOW PACE OF LIFE. IN THE MORNINGS DALÍ PAINTED, AND GALA WOULD ROW OUT TO SEA TO CATCH A LOBSTER OR SOME FISH FOR LUNCH.

The Persistence of Memory

Gala was out at the cinema when Dalí painted *The Persistence of Memory*. When she returned, he asked her to sit down and close her eyes. After a dramatic countdown she was allowed to open her eyes, and Dalí unveiled his canvas. Gala's opinion was that, "No one can forget it once he has seen it." The melting clocks seem unsettling, but there is a simplicity to this iconic image. It captures the spirit of their home at Port Lligat where, according to Dalí, time slowed or "melted," and reflects the comfort Dalí found in Gala, as he explains: "Gala ... succeeded in building for me a shell ... within myself I continue to grow old in the soft and the supersoft. And the day I painted the watches, I painted them soft." The image is also about some rather stinky cheese. Before painting the watches, Dalí ate some very runny Camembert, and the melting cheese is manifested in the melting watches.

The play between soft and hard forms is something that fascinated Dalí. *The Secret Life of Salvador Dalí* opens with Dalí pontificating on the horror of the "utterly amorphous character" of spinach, which he contrasts with the hard "armour" of the lobster. The witty Surrealist liked to play with people's expectations, creating public art – which was typically made from immutable metals – out of edible, fluffy dough. At the dinner table he would disgust guests by eating animal bones: "How wonderful to crunch a bird's tiny skull. How can one eat brains any other way?" More than a gag, his melting clock has a philosophical significance. For many years, time had been a fashionable subject: Albert Einstein and Henri Bergson questioned the validity of clock time, and Dalí's unctuous clock has the fluidity of Bergson's durée, or "real" time.

Madness and Dalí's Paranoiac-Critical Method

Dalí's understanding of a "surreal" reality was like a constantly gathering force. He first identified it as something natural, like the Great Rocks that laid bare fantastic forms, and then later he attached Freud's unconscious world to his theory. In his account of painting *The Persistence of Memory*, he describes having a vision. In the 1930s Dalí developed the idea of a paranoiac-critical method: to unlock the marvellous, he now argued that one had to be in a frenzied state. He likened himself to a madman who hallucinates and uncovers multiple realities, commenting that "the only difference between me and a madman is that I am not mad." Breton championed the potential of Dalí's approach, but he found Dalí's glorification of madness insensitive.

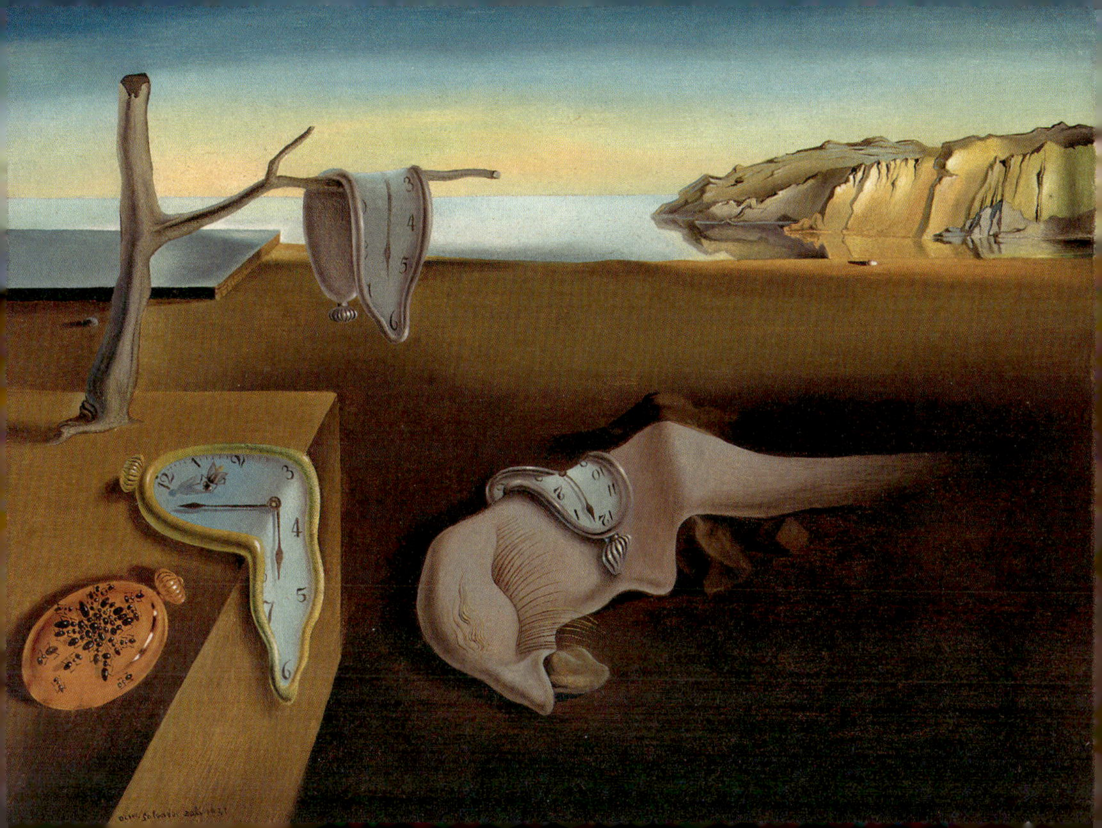

A Trial Turns into a Striptease

Breton was becoming increasingly concerned by some of Dalí's views. Dalí could be very cruel, and he was advocating values that were uncomfortably close to Hitler's fascist ideals. The final straw for Breton was Dalí's painting *The Enigma of William Tell* (c. 1933). In this work, Vladimir Lenin – Communist leader and hero to the Surrealists – is portrayed as a pathetic figure, stripped semi-naked and crouching on the ground.

In February 1934 Breton called Dalí to a "trial" to justify his role in Surrealism. Dalí made a mockery of the whole procedure. Wearing layers of woolly jumpers and with a thermometer in his mouth, he turned up declaring that he was sick. When a question was put to him, he took off a layer of clothing and checked his temperature. Dalí's behaviour enraged some, and had others in fits of laughter. While he played court jester, he argued his case, famously stating at one point: "I myself am Surrealism." Dalí's point was that if Surrealism prioritized unconscious thought, it would be a contradiction to censor or forbid unconscious thoughts. In the end the Child King managed to weave his way out of trouble; Breton did not formally expel him from the Surrealist group until 1939.

A Trip to America

By 1934, Dalí had become impatient: the Surrealist trial was an embarrassing affair, he was penniless, and he hankered after success and fame. In America there was growing interest in his work, and so the Child King stamped his foot and a secret patron (who turned out to be Picasso) paid for his trip to America. The trip was like an ongoing Surrealist drama. Terrified at sea, Dalí made the whole cross-Atlantic adventure strapped into his bunk bed with his paintings tied to his fingers or clothing by string. Carrying one of his enormously long baguettes, Dalí disembarked and was greeted by a horde of reporters. He ceremoniously "broke bread," and shared the baguette with his bemused audience.

Dalí found a surreal beauty in the New York landscape: "It rose before me, verdigris, pink, and creamy-white. It looked like an immense Gothic Roquefort cheese. I love Roquefort." In his writings he relishes America as a place for the absurd, where "cypress trees grow from the walls of the empty skyscrapers," and he links Surrealist thinking with Hollywood slapstick, and the "forerunners of the irrational – Mack Sennett, Harry Langdon, and, you too, unforgettable Buster Keaton."

At the opening night of his exhibition at the Julien Levy Gallery, Dalí amused and mesmerized New Yorkers. His exhibition was a huge success. Twelve paintings were sold, and they reached far higher prices than Dalí had ever commanded in Europe. It turned into an unrelenting promotional tour, with Dalí seizing every opportunity to advance his position. He gave a series of high-profile lectures; on January 11, 1935, he talked at the Museum of Modern Art on "Surrealist Painting and Paranoiac Images." By the end of his trip he was a New York celebrity. And he loved every minute of it.

Prodigal Son or Political Coward?

On his return to Spain, Dalí visited his father in Figueres. He had not seen his family since 1929. According to his aunt, who was present, it was a very emotional meeting that ended well. However, worried that civil war was about to break out, Dalí did not stay long in Spain. Before he left the country he painted *Soft Construction with Boiled Beans (Premonition of Civil War)*, which depicted Spain, to quote Dalí, as "a vast human body breaking into monstrous excrescences of arms and legs tearing at one another in a delirium of autostrangulation." Dalí's position on the Spanish Civil War is confusing. Initially he supported the revolutionaries – at the outbreak of the war, his friend and muse Lorca was killed by the fascists. However, later, he changed sides and supported the fascist government, which outraged friends and the art world alike. The situation in Spain was complicated: friends and family members were pitted against each other. As a member of the middle class, Dalí's father was targeted by the revolutionaries, and the whole family was appallingly treated. His sister Ana María was imprisoned and tortured by the communists, and his father's house was ransacked.

Characteristically, Dalí was cowardly and avoided dealing with the situation. When he and Gala fled Spain, they carried both the Nationalist and Republican flags, and whichever side approached, they hoisted the appropriate flag. Dalí and Gala did not return to Spain until after World War II. Breton despised their cowardly behaviour. Dalí was not worried. He had other things on his mind.

Soft Construction with Boiled Beans (Premonition of Civil War)
Salvador Dalí, 1936

Oil on canvas
39⅓ × 39⅜ in (99.9 × 100 cm)
Philadelphia Museum of Art,
The Louise and Walter Arensberg Collection 1950

Lobster Telephone
Salvador Dalí, 1936

Plastic, painted plaster and mixed media
7 × 13 × 7 in (17.8 × 33 × 17.8 cm)

The Surreal Object

The Surrealists were opening up alternative modes of expression. Breton had been thinking about the possibilities of a surreal object for many years. Originally his idea came from a dream – he remembers a fantastic book, with pages of thick black cloth, and a spine bearing the shape of a wooden gnome. At the time, he wrote, "I would like to put some objects such as this into circulation." Later he generously identified Dalí as the master of the surreal object.

Dalí always wanted to amuse his audience, and his surreal objects are playful and provocative. Often there is a sexual undercurrent; indeed Dalí's plan was to create "animatable objects, openly erotic, I mean destined to procure, by indirect means, a particular sexual emotion." Playing the prankster, he clipped a pink lobster onto a telephone. The *Lobster Telephone* points to the uncanny relationship between objects. The components of a telephone receiver and the lobster are the same – both have a head, a body, and a bottom, and, of course, Dalí relished that we talk into the lobster's reproductive organs.

British art collector Edward James bought a number of lobster telephones for his extravagant home. In the 1930s Dalí broke into the British art scene. In the summer of 1936 he astounded viewers at the London International Surrealist Exhibition when he turned up to give a lecture dressed in a diving suit with Russian wolfhounds by his side. Somewhat dramatically, he became trapped in the airless helmet, and was rescued by the young poet David Gascoyne. Emerging, struggling for breath, Dalí announced: "I just wanted to show that I was 'plunging deeply' into the human mind." The next day, Dalí made front-page news.

Refining Double Vision

In the 1930s and 1940s there was a shift in Dalí, as art historian Dawn Ades describes: "The period of organic abstraction in Surrealist painting [with its references to] 'inaccessible mutilations, of unrealizable sanguinary osmoses, of loose visceral torn holes, of rocks' hair, and catastrophic emigrations' is over."

Focused on his paranoiac-critical method, Dalí published his treatise *The Conquest of the Irrational* (1935) and perfected the technique of double imagery. The painting *Slave Market with the Disappearing Bust of Voltaire* (1940) is perhaps his most sophisticated expression. In it, two completely different realities coexist. In one world we see a semi-nude Gala looking over at a crowd of people, including two women dressed in seventeenth-century costume. In the second world, the two costumed women and the arched doorway coalesce to form the bust of the writer Voltaire. The double takes are certainly clever. But it is almost as if Dalí had backed himself into a corner with his paranoiac-critical method. Did he endlessly want to create double images? In the 1940s he searched for new subject matter.

Dalí also diversified. After meeting the famous interior decorator Jean-Michel Frank, he moved into furniture design, producing the gilt-framed Leda Chair (the chair first appears in an earlier painting, *Woman with Head of Roses*). A perky piece, Dalí plays with the components: the "arm" of the chair becomes a sinuous human arm, and the three chair legs totter on delicate high-heeled shoes. Dalí also ventured into jewellery design. His most famous piece is probably the Ruby Lips brooch. Reflecting that, "Poets of the ages, of all lands, write of ruby lips and teeth like pearls," he makes lips from real rubies, and a set of teeth from small round pearls. It is extravagant humour.

The language of the commercial world echoed Dalí's paranoiac-critical method. A good advert will transform an ordinary object and make it seem magnificent. Dalí also imbues his objects with a latent sexuality – a technique that advertising certainly exploits. In fact, he became paranoid that businesses were stealing his original way of thinking: "... the window displays of a great majority of shops ... were visibly under the surrealist influence, and ... under my personal influence. But the constant drama of my influence lies in the fact that once launched, it escapes from my hands, and I can no longer carnalize it, or even profit by it."

Slave Market with the Disappearing Bust of Voltaire
Salvador Dalí, 1940

Oil on canvas
18¼ × 25¾ in (46.5 × 65.5 cm)
Salvador Dalí Museum, St Petersburg, Florida

Bonwit Teller Store

In America, Dalí's celebrity continued to grow. In 1939 he was commissioned to dress the windows for Bonwit Teller, a department store with, as *Time* magazine reported, "a reputation for having Manhattan's screwiest window displays." When it hired the Surrealist superstar, the company promised Dalí complete artistic control. This turned out not to be the case, and the Child King threw an epic tantrum that made front-page news.

Dalí came up with the rather hackneyed theme of "Day and Night." However, his deathly design was provocative. A mangy, almost rotting mannequin, with green nails and matted red hair, stood by a bath filled with water, from which three mannequin arms emerged. The wax dummies were truly sinister: their bodies had yellowed over time, and their hair had been sourced from real corpses. Taxidermy littered the exhibit: the bath was lined with the fleece of a black Persian lamb. A nightmarish bed stood on four buffalo legs and was overlooked by the buffalo's head, which held a bloody pigeon in its mouth.

When the store opened at 9.30 am, people complained. The shop management decided to replace Dalí's diabolical mannequins with its own models in modern dress. Dalí was outraged: "So I dashed into the window to rearrange it, so that my name, signed in the window, should not be dishonoured, I was never so surprised as when the bath tub shot through the window when I pushed it, and I was thereafter most confused." Dalí was arrested and thrown into jail with "[the] drunks and professional bums, who vomited and fought among themselves with an admirable optimism." Dalí's defence was that he had been "hired to do a work of art" and he didn't want his name "associated with typical window dressing." Judge Louis Brodsky was forgiving; as he put it, "these are some of the privileges that an artist with a temperament seems to enjoy."

The affair was fantastic promotion for the artist and indeed the high-end fashion store. Dalí became the figurehead Surrealist, as writer Henry Miller describes: "Surrealism, if you should happen to ask anyone off-hand, means Salvador Dalí." In the midst of the Bonwit Teller ruckus, Dalí was asked to design the Dream of Venus pavilion for the Amusement Area of the World's Fair in New York that year.

BONWIT
TELLER

America

Dalí's refusal to engage with social and political issues angered other Surrealists. Europe was in turmoil, the civil war had destroyed Spain, and militant dictators controlled Germany and Italy. In 1939 the world was on the brink of another world war. And Dalí? He just went on the run. On September 1, Hitler invaded Poland, and Dalí scuttled off to the southwest of France. As he self-indulgently recounts: "I studied my winter campaign, trying to plan it in such a way as to combine the possibility of a Nazi invasion with gastronomical possibilities ... I finally put my finger ... on a neuralgic point of French cooking: Bordeaux. That would be one of the last places the Germans reached if, as seemed highly improbable, they should win .... Moreover Bordeaux naturally meant Bordeaux wine, jugged hare, duck liver aux raisins, duck aux oranges, Arcachon claire-oysters ... Arcachon. I've got it."

The Surrealists probably could have dealt with Dalí's cowardice, but he stepped over the line when he found a subject, and a drama, in the savage dictator Adolf Hitler. His painting *The Enigma of Hitler* had presented the Führer almost sympathetically, as a sort of mysterious presence. In 1940 Dalí fled to America, which remained his home until the end of World War II. He clearly felt comfortable there. In *Poetry of America – The Cosmic Athletes* (1943) he blends the American landscape with scenes from his beloved Spain: the tower from the Pichot estate and the seascape of Cadaqués are placed in the American desert. Celebrating an iconic American product, he puts a Coca-Cola bottle in the foreground of the picture. It is a radical gesture that anticipates Pop Art, and Andy Warhol's endorsement of America's top brand:

> What's great about this country is that America started the tradition where the richest consumers buy essentially the same things as the poorest. You can be watching TV and see Coca-Cola, and you know that the President drinks Coke, Liz Taylor drinks Coke, and just think, you can drink Coke, too. A Coke is a Coke and no amount of money can get you a better Coke than the one the bum on the corner is drinking. All the Cokes are the same and all the Cokes are good. Liz Taylor knows it, the President knows it, the bum knows it, and you know it.

YOUR ELBOW IS AS EDIBLE AS THE HEEL OF A LOAF OF BREAD.
YOUR LIPS ARE AS EDIBLE AS PEELED MUSCAT GRAPES.
Nuits-St-Georges

Surreal Business

Dalí became a commercial phenomenon in America. He went into business with fashion designer Elsa Schiaparelli, and came up with some outrageous clothes: an inkwell hat, a shoe hat, and a dress imprinted with a chest of drawers. He designed covers for *Vogue*, and created the logo for the Spanish lollipop company, Chupa Chups; he had the brilliant idea of putting the logo on top of the lolly so that it was fully visible. A bankable commodity, Dalí started selling his aura indiscriminately, appearing in ads endorsing indigestion tablets and chocolate. The Surrealists hated Dalí's obsession with money. Breton made a brilliant anagram of his name, calling him Avida Dollars (a homophone of the French phrase meaning "eager for dollars").

Surreal Pleasure

In New York, Dalí continued to paint, but also spent a lot of time writing. He published his autobiography, *The Secret Life of Salvador Dalí* (1942), which is more fiction than fact, and he wrote the novel *Hidden Faces* (1944). The latter is rich in Surrealist imagery; in one scene the main character, the Count of Grandsailles, sits at the dinner table staring at the reflection of his dinner guests in his silverware, which reminds one of Dalí's fabulous mirrored fingernails.

Dalí thought he was advancing Surrealism just by living it. The absurd played into every facet of his life – his dress, eating habits and even relationships. Dalí had always admired the comedian Harpo Marx's slapstick humour, and they became friends around 1937. Dalí had met his match. One Christmas, Dalí sent Harpo a harp strung with barbed wire, and Harpo replied with wit, sending a photograph of himself playing the harp with bandaged fingers.

Eating dinner was like a theatrical event. Dalí had queer tastes: his favourite meal was lobster and chocolate sauce. He also had an appetite for tiny birds, which he would eat whole, with their guts and feathers. One of his muses, Isabelle Dufresne (later to rename herself Ultra Violet and join Andy Warhol's factory), tells of a bizarre night out with Dalí, which consisted of "tongue touching," some preposterous conversation, and a lavish dinner.

The modern-day Chupa Chups lollipop still reflects Dalí's design.

Dalí and Hollywood

Hollywood had always fascinated Dalí, and he was desperate to work there. In 1944 Alfred Hitchcock asked him to contribute the background for a dream sequence in his latest film, *Spellbound*. The film brought psychoanalytic theory to the murder/mystery genre, focusing on the idea that repressed emotion can trigger neurosis. The Dalí name was a valuable asset as it inevitably meant free press coverage – Hitchcock's studio noted that Dalí had appeared in *Life* magazine six times in the previous year. Dalí was not simply a commercial choice. Hitchcock liked the artist's crisp dream landscapes. He hated the film cliché that "all dreams in the movies are blurred," and thought that Dalí would bring clarity. They planned the dream scene to look hyper-realistic. As with some of his previous collaborations, Dalí felt compromised, and many of the scenes he had worked on were cut. However, the final sequence is definitely Dalíesque, with looming shadows, dropping perspectives, and lots of eyeballs. At one point a pair of giant scissors cuts through a painted eye, obviously referencing the horrific scene from *Un Chien Andalou*.

Return to Spain

After World War II, Dalí returned to his homeland, Spain. He sent Franco a telegram congratulating him for clearing Spain of "destructive forces." Why did he do this? Was it just a cold opportunism? It was a cataclysmic move. The art world was disgusted, and the locals of Port Lligat turned against him. He was forced to leave the village for a while. Dalí's muse, Carlos Lozano, describes the scene: "Death threats appeared on the whitewashed walls around Port Lligat and the chair Dalí regularly occupied at his favourite restaurant, the Via Veneto in Barcelona, was blown up. His first thought when George Harrison materialized over the garden wall had been that he was an assassin."

Dalí's insensitivity was unrelenting. When he moved into his father's house, he ordered Gala to park their Cadillac outside the house. Since very few people owned a car in the village, it was a flagrant statement of superiority. Perhaps it was also a defiant act against his father but despite all this, his father welcomed him home. Salvador Dalí Cusí warmed to Gala, and he loved riding in her black Cadillac. In September 1950, he died of prostate cancer. Dalí did not attend his father's funeral. Allegedly, the Tramontana wind raged that day.

The villagers were less forgiving. For years they had endured the oppressive Franco dictatorship while Dalí partied in New York. In the 1950s locals found out that Dalí was meeting with Franco, and they pleaded with him to speak to the General about the appalling poverty in the area, but the sycophant reported that everything was well in his hometown. In fact, Dalí continued to herald Franco at press conferences, and even painted a portrait of Franco's daughter.

Dalí and Celebrity Culture

After the war, Dalí and Gala's life followed a regular pattern: Spring, summer, and autumn were spent in Port Lligat, and in winter they entertained in Paris and New York. In New York, admirers met at Dalí's suite in the Hotel Regina, and in Paris he hosted his "Court of Miracles" at the Hotel Meurice from 5 until 8 pm. Dalí had become a cultural phenomenon. The Beatles, themselves a world sensation, sought him out; George Harrison jumped the wall at Dalí's home in Port Lligat and, supposedly, begged for a hair from Dalí's moustache. There are many stories about the sale of hairs from this celebrated moustache: one account says that Gala once pulled a hair and demanded $300,000 for it. The rich and famous wanted the Dalí endorsement. And Dalí? He was equally star-obsessed: he met Andy Warhol at the Factory, and dined with Francis Crick and James Watson shortly after their discovery of the structure of DNA. The difficulty was that Dalí demanded adoration, as he said, "I am Da-lí; Da-lí. You must bring me presents. I adore presents," and the great and good were not always so taken with him. Freud thought him a fanatic, and Crick and Watson were overwhelmed by his exuberant (perhaps idiotic) behaviour.

Dalí dipped into the celebrity world, but in his later years he preferred to be surrounded by adoring groupies. The Child King played monarch to misfits, as friend Carlos Lozano tells: "He was a genius, but a genius cannot be a genius all the time and the court were there to colour the background."

Dalí with Andy Warhol at Laurent Restaurant, New York, 1978.
Photo by Christopher Makos
www.makostudio.com

The Queen's Castle

Dalí and Gala had an open marriage. Gala's mantra was to live her life as a "constant explosion." In 1963, at 69 years old, she became involved with William Rotlein, a young homeless drug addict. After attempting to "save" him she seems to have got bored. Increasingly Gala and Dalí lived separate lives. In 1969 Dalí bought Púbol Castle for Gala. It became a refuge from the busy social life that went on at Port Lligat, and a love nest for her string of paramours. Dalí was allowed to visit only if he had received a written invitation. He would always arrive bearing gifts. In 1973 Gala started a new relationship with Jeff Fenholt, who had the leading role in the musical *Jesus Christ Superstar.* Infatuated (some say senile), Gala bought him a million-dollar house, lavished him with gifts, and met his demands for cash.

Dalí's affairs were more esoteric. He had a long relationship with Amanda Lear, a hip model and later pop star whose sex at birth is debated. According to Lear, they had a spiritual marriage. For a few years she was the Princess of Port Lligat.

Dalí with Amanda Lear
c. 1966, France.

THE INNER COURT
ACCORDING TO HIS BIOGRAPHERS, DALÍ'S COURT WAS FULL OF FRAUDSTERS. BUT DALÍ DIDN'T CARE. HE PLAYED UP TO THEIR ASPIRATIONS AND FANTASIES. REFLECTING DALÍ'S LAZINESS AND HIS LACK OF EFFORT WITH PEOPLE, MOST COURTIERS WERE GIVEN GENERIC NAMES. A FEW INDIVIDUALS WHO WERE CLOSER TO HIM KEPT THEIR OWN NAMES, OR WERE AT LEAST GIVEN SPECIFIC NICKNAMES.
I AM A MONARCHIST, AN APOSTOLIC, AND A ROMAN CATHOLIC. YOU RECOGNIZE THE TIE-PIN OF ALFONSO XIII, NO DOUBT?
ONE OF THE FEW PEOPLE WHOM DALÍ REFERRE
TO BY NAME WAS AMANDA LEAR. IT IS SAID T
AMANDA WAS BORN A MAN, BUT SHE ALWAYS
DENIED THIS. INCREDIBLY GLAMOROUS, SHE D
STARS SUCH AS DAVID BOWIE AND BRYAN FER
"LOUIS XIV," OR NANITA KALASCHNIKOFF, WAS ONE OF DALÍ'S FAVOURITE COURTIERS. SHE WAS A RICH AND BEAUTIFUL SOCIALITE.
HANDSOME BOYS WERE NAMED "SAINT SEBASTIAN."
EAST ASIAN PEOPLE WERE CALLED "RED GUARDS."
THE POSH AND WELL-BRED WERE CALLED "FILLETS OF SOLE."

FREE LOVE

COURT LIFE WAS RITUALIZED. THE MONARCH COULD BE IDENTIFIED BY HIS REGAL TIE-PIN, AND "COURTIERS ... WERE TREATED WITH A CERTAIN DEGREE OF SCORN, ACCORDING TO THEIR IMPORTANCE." THEIR PHILOSOPHY, IF THERE WAS ONE, WAS BASED LOOSELY ON "FREE LOVE."

DALÍ INSISTED THAT GALA WAS THE MOST IMPORTANT PERSON IN HIS LIFE, BUT THEIR RELATIONSHIP WAS UNUSUAL. THEY HAD AN OPEN MARRIAGE AND COULD BE VERY CRUEL TO ONE ANOTHER.

BLONDES WERE NAMED "GINESTRA," AFTER THE YELLOW SPRING FLOWER THAT GROWS ACROSS THE MEDITERRANEAN SHORE.

JEFF FENHOLT

DALÍ REFERRED TO TWINS JOHN AND DENNIS MYERS AS "DIOSCURI," BROTHERS IN GREEK MYTHOLOGY.

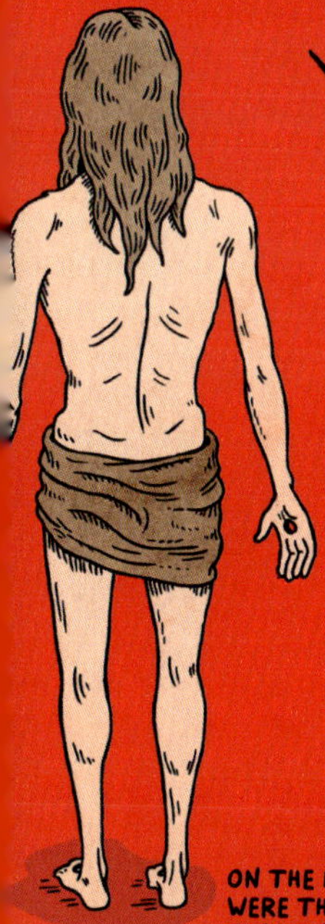

ON THE BASIS THAT THEY WERE THIN AND PALE, FASHION MODELS WERE REFERRED TO AS "CHRISTS."

A Ruthless Pursuit

Dalí had always been deeply impressionable. In later years he was inspired by modern science, and in particular atomic theory. To quote him: "Today the external world – that of physics – has transcended that of psychology. Today my father is Dr. Heisenberg." Reflecting Werner Heisenberg's pioneering work in atomic theory, the *Exploding Raphaelesque Head* vaporizes matter into spiral particles. Later Dalí identified the spiral form as the "rhinoceros horn." A rhinomania took over Dalí: he painted rhino horns, made a film about the rhino, and professes to "see" horns everywhere – in earlier paintings, and also in the Great Rocks of Cadaqués.

This grandiose mixture of atomic theory, classicism, and rhinomania was insensitively handled, and was also untimely. By linking atomic energy with a classical order (and Raphael), Dalí portrays atomic energy as a serene, malevolent force, and yet World War II had revealed the horrifying power of atomic energy. When the first bomb hit Hiroshima, 70,000 people were instantly vaporized. Dalí remembers that day: "The atomic bomb of August 6, 1945 shook me seismically. Thenceforth, the atom was my favourite food for thought. Many of the landscapes painted in this period express the great fear inspired in me by the announcement of that explosion." It is almost as if the Child King again sensed mileage in a fraught subject, and feasted on it. Even the year before Hiroshima, the writer George Orwell had observed, "[Dalí] is as anti-social as a flea."

Dalí with a rhino
From the *Chaos and Creation* show filmed for CBS, 1956.
Photo by Philippe Halsman

Exploding Raphaelesque Head
Salvador Dalí, 1951

Spirituality

A new mysticism pervades Dalí's late painting. When he returned to Europe after the war, Dalí reaffirmed his commitment to Catholicism, and went to great lengths to arrange a meeting with the Pope, who blessed him. It is difficult to say what a Papal blessing meant to him. Perhaps the needy Child King was simply searching for validation? It could be that religion was just another potent subject matter. In his writings he irreverently assumes the role of God, to quote: "I, Dalí, shall use my work to demonstrate the unity of the universe, by showing the spirituality of all substance."

The painting *Christ of St John of the Cross* has the scale of a grand religious work. Dalí's intention was to capture the "mystical beauty of Christ." He locates the crucifix in Port Lligat. The view is from his front door which looks out over the bay, with Gala's yellow fishing boat moored in the foreground. It is a peaceful crucifixion: there are no nails on the cross, and no blood is shed. In the Bible, Jesus cries out: "My God, why hast thou forsaken me?," but Dalí's Christ is not alone. The Father's presence is implied in the extraordinary perspective. Christ is drawn from a position of height, implying that the Father is watching over his son from heaven. The implied intimacy between God and his son perhaps reflects Dalí's reconciliation with his own father.

A tour-de-force, the painting is a synthesis of ideas and interests. Previously reconciling surrealism with a hard-edged realism, Dalí now merged the spiritual with a scientific objectivity. He called his new faith Nuclear Mysticism. The most explicit reference to nuclear physics is the shadow around Christ's head, which is meant to signify "the nucleus of the atom." With the composition based on strict mathematical proportions, the Godly realm sits above a detailed landscape. Christ's body is based on meticulous analyses. After an exhausting casting, the Hollywood stuntman Russell Saunders was hired to model for Christ; Saunders was strapped to a gantry so that Dalí could fathom how muscles respond to the force of gravity.

The combination of ideals ends in a very unusual crucifixion scene. Typically, realist-driven representations emphasize the physical pain that Christ endured. By instead foregrounding Christ's beauty, and "unpinning" him from the cross, Dalí creates a Christ who could be mistaken for a champion high diver. The spiritual slightly ventures into the kitsch.

DALÍ AND GALA WOULD DRESS UP IN WHITE CLOAKS AND WALK DOWN THE PATH IN THE MOONLIGHT.
THE LATER DESIGN OF THE BEDROOM REFLECTED DALÍ'S GROWING MEGALOMANIA: A MAJESTIC EAGLE SAT ON TOP OF THE GILT BED FRAME, AND THE BEDSPREADS WERE OPULENT.
THE CAP DE CREUS IS LOCATED ON THE MOST EASTERN POINT OF MAINLAND SPAIN. DALÍ POSITIONED A MIRROR TO REFLECT THE MORNING SUN SO THAT HE COULD BE THE FIRST IN SPAIN TO EXPERIENCE THE DAWN.
DALÍ BUILT A PATHWAY ALONG THE COAST, WHICH HE CALLED THE VIA LACTEA ("MILKY WAY"). HE LAID SLATE WALLS AND PLANTED WILD LAVENDER AND BROOM.
THE WARM YELLOW OF THE SOFA IS LIKE A RAY OF MEDITERRANEAN SUN.
THROUGHOUT T HOUSE, WINDOW FRAME THE EPIC LANDSCAPE, WH DALÍ PROCLAIME "THERE IS A GEOLOGICAL CA IT IS A UNIQUE PLANETARY CAS

DALÍ AT HOME, PORT LLIGAT, 1930–82

DALÍ AND GALA TRANSFORMED THEIR MODEST FISHERMAN'S COTTAGE INTO A GRAND RESIDENCE. THE INTERIOR IS RESTRAINED. THERE ARE MOMENTS OF SURREAL PLEASURE: YOU ARE GREETED BY A POLAR BEAR WEARING NECKLACES AND HOLDING JEWELLED CANES, AND THE LAYOUT IS MAZE-LIKE, WITH SPLIT FLOORS, NARROW, LABYRINTHINE CORRIDORS, AND A DEAD END. HOWEVER, THE PERVADING SENSE IS CALM AND PEACEFUL.

THE ROOMS ARE WELCOMING, WITH WHITE-WASHED AND BRIGHTLY COLOURED CARPETS. THE FURNITURE IS AUSTERE AND CLASSICAL, AND COLOUR IS USED MODESTLY – OFTEN THE INTERIORS ARE HARMONIZED AROUND ONE CENTRAL COLOUR. THE OUTSIDE AREA WAS DEVELOPED AFTER THE WAR, AND HAS A VERY DIFFERENT SPIRIT. HERE, OUTLANDISH EXHIBITIONISM MIXES WITH DESPERATION AS WE SEE AN OLD MAN'S ATTEMPT TO IMPRESS AND SHOCK THE YOUTHFUL.

The Largest Surrealist Museum in the World

Dalí's grandest creation is the Theatre-Museum in Figueres. It is the ultimate Surrealist entertainment. According to Amanda Lear, Dalí wanted "fantasy, disorder, and a total absence of pomposity." It is a pleasure dome that houses Dalí's fantasies: from the bear by the stairs to the hallucinatory Mae West room. There is a mix of art, antique curiosities, biological wonders, funfare attractions, and Dalí's collection of precious jewels.

In the Mae West room, Dalí realizes a "double reality" within a living space. The works of art and pieces of furniture are arranged to create a three-dimensional illusion of Mae West's face: the two paintings form her eyes, the drapes become her hair, the sofa is her lips, and the fireplace her nose. The sofa is the focal point of the room. Mae West's lips mesmerized Dalí and embodied the essence of the Hollywood star. We are invited to sit down on the lips ... characteristically, Dalí has laden the experience with humour.

The museum opened on September 28,1974. With circus animals and majorettes, it was more like a funfair than an international art event. Holding a spikenard (the flower that his mother grew on their balcony), Dalí arrived with Lear while Gala searched in the crowd for the singer Jeff Fenholt, with whom she was by then having an affair. The somewhat disastrous opening reflected Dalí's fallen reputation.

Financial Scandals

The GalaDalí beast had become insatiable and their financial situation was ridiculous. In order to avoid taxes, Gala transported money round the world, brazenly walking through customs with suitcases full of bank notes. They had bank accounts in Switzerland and stashes of cash round the house. In the mid-1960s Dalí started signing blank sheets of paper. Originally the idea was that publishers would add prints later, but the sheets ended up being sold illegally, and forgeries swamped the market. And Dalí? He wasn't bothered: "I have already been paid for what they offered for the work." In 1975 America's Internal Revenue Service launched an investigation into Dalí's tax returns.

Mae West room at Dalí's Theatre-Museum
Salvador Dalí, c. 1974

Various materials and sizes
Teatre-Museu Dalí, Figueres
Based on a painting called *Mae West's Face which May Be Used as a Surrealist Apartment* (9934/35)

Surreal Endings

Gala's affair with Jeff Fenholt had preyed on Dalí; he had worried that Gala might leave him. Supposedly, Gala subdued her fretful husband with prescription drugs, which caused Parkinson-like symptoms; the hand tremors left him unable to paint. It was the start of a wretched end.

On June 10, 1982, Gala died in their home at Port Lligat. Knowing that Gala wanted to be laid to rest at Púbol Castle, and worried that the Spanish authorities might insist on burial at her place of death, a final Surrealist drama was performed. Her corpse was bundled into her beloved Cadillac. Sat upright beside her nurse, she was driven back to Púbol where she was laid to rest in the castle crypt, wearing her favourite red Dior dress and signature black velvet bow. Dalí ordered that a bunch of spikenards be laid on her coffin; he could not bear to go to her funeral. A few hours later he went to her tomb and pathetically boasted to his cousin, "Look, I'm not crying."

Without Gala, Dalí lost his will to live. According to long-standing friend and patron Mara Albaretto, "Whatever their differences, whatever their rows, they were vital to each other. Gala was the mainstay, the will power. And now she was gone. Dalí felt like a child abandoned by his mother." Dalí shut himself into Gala's bedroom and refused to eat. One night a fire broke out, and Dalí was very badly burnt. He survived and lived for a number of years, but it was a miserable existence. In 1988, his health deteriorated further and he became obsessed by the desire to see the King of Spain, Juan Carlos. The Child King's final whim was granted when on December 5 the King visited him in hospital. He died a few weeks later, on January 23, 1989.

Dalí had organized for his afterlife. His body was embalmed, his moustache waxed, and, dressed in a simple beige tunic, he was entombed in the cupola at his museum. The place of burial remains a somewhat contentious subject. Originally Dalí had wanted to be beside his Queen, but in the last few weeks of his life the plan changed. It seems fitting that the Child King rests in his own personal mausoleum, with his treasure.

Glossary

ANTHROPOMORPHIC Described or thought of as being like human beings in appearance, behavior, etc.; considering animals, objects, etc., as having human qualities.

AUSTERITY A simple and plain quality; a situation in which there is not much money and it is spent only on things that are necessary.

AVANT-GARDE A group of people who develop new and often very surprising ideas in art, literature, etc.

BIZARRE Very unusual or strange; strikingly out of the ordinary; odd, extravagant, or eccentric in style or mode.

DETERIORATE To make inferior in quality or value; to disintegrate; to become impaired in quality, functioning, or condition.

EMBELLISH To decorate (something) by adding special details and features; to make (something) more appealing or attractive.

ESOTERIC Only taught to or understood by members of a special group; hard to understand; limited to a small number of people; of special, rare, or unusual interest.

FLAMBOYANT Marked by or given to strikingly elaborate or colorful display or behavior; having a very noticeable quality that attracts a lot of attention.

HYPERBOLE Language that describes something as better or worse than it really is; extravagant exaggeration.

IMPRESSIONISM A theory or practice in painting, especially among French painters of about 1870 of depicting the natural appearances of objects by means of dabs or strokes of primary unmixed colors in order to simulate actual reflected light; the depiction (as in literature) of scene, emotion, or character by details intended to achieve a vividness or effectiveness more by evoking subjective and sensory impressions than by recreating an objective reality.

INFANTILIZE To treat someone like a baby; to make or keep someone childish.

MEGALOMANIA A condition or mental illness that causes people to think that they have great or unlimited power or importance; delusions of grandeur and omnipotence.

MORPHOLOGY A study of structure or form; the external structure of rocks in relation to the development of erosional forms or topographic feature.

NATURALISM Realism in art or literature; a style of art or literature that shows people and things as they actually are.

PARANOID Of, relating to, or suffering from a mental illness that causes you to falsely believe that people are trying to harm you; having or showing an unreasonable feeling that people are trying to harm you, do not like you, etc.

PSYCHOANALYSIS A method of explaining and treating mental and emotional problems by having the patient talk about personal experiences, early childhood, dreams, feelings, memories, etc.

REALISM The theory or practice of fidelity in art and literature to nature or to real life and to accurate representation without idealization; concern for fact or reality and rejection of the impractical and visionary.

SURREAL Very strange or unusual; having the quality and irrational reality or logic of a dream; unbelievable; fantastic.

SURREALISM A twentieth-century art form in which an artist or writer combines unrelated images or events in a very strange and dreamlike way.

TYRANNY Oppressive power; cruel and unfair treatment by people with power over others; an oppressive, harsh, or unjust act.

For More Information

Art Institute of Chicago
111 South Michigan Avenue
Chicago, IL 60603-6404
Website: http://www.artic.edu
The Art Institute of Chicago collects, preserves, and interprets works of art of the highest quality, representing the world's diverse artistic traditions, for the inspiration and education of the public and in accordance with the profession's highest ethical standards and practices.

The Dali Museum
One Dali Boulevard
St. Petersburg, FL 33701
(727) 823-3767
Website: http://thedali.org
The Dali Museum shares an expertly curated collection of Salvador Dali works to delight and educate visitors and provide unique inspiration for events, programs, and special exhibits that allow it to serve as an active resource in the cultural life of its community and the world at large.

The Getty
1200 Getty Center Drive
Los Angeles, CA 90049-1679
(310) 440-7300
Website: http://www.getty.edu
The J. Paul Getty Trust is a cultural and philanthropic institution dedicated to the presentation, conservation, and interpretation of the world's artistic legacy. The Getty is dedicated to the proposition that works of art are windows onto the world's diverse and intertwined histories, mirrors of humanity's innate imagination and creativity, and inspiration to envision the future.

The Museum of Modern Art (MoMA)
11 West 53rd Street
New York, NY 10019
(212) 708-9400
Website: https://www.moma.org
Founded in 1929 as an educational institution, The Museum of Modern Art is dedicated to being the foremost museum of modern art in the world. Through the leadership of its Trustees and staff, The Museum of Modern Art manifests this

commitment by establishing, preserving, and documenting a permanent collection of the highest order that reflects the vitality, complexity, and unfolding patterns of modern and contemporary art and by presenting exhibitions and educational programs of unparalleled significance. Central to The Museum of Modern Art's mission is the encouragement of an ever-deeper understanding and enjoyment of modern and contemporary art by the diverse local, national, and international audiences that it serves.

Websites

Because of the changing nature of internet links, Rosen Publishing has developed an online list of websites related to the subject of this book. This site is updated regularly. Please use this link to access this list:

http://www.rosenlinks.com/LGA/dali

For Further Reading

Descharnes, Robert, and Gilles Neret. *Dalí: The Paintings.* Cologne, Germany: Taschen, 2013.

Descharnes, Robert, and Gilles Neret. *Salvador Dalí, 1904-1989* (2 vols.). Cologne, Germany: Taschen, 2007.

Dalí, Salvador. *Les Diners de Gala.* Cologne, Germany: Taschen, 2016.

Dalí, Salvador. *The Secret Life of Salvador Dalí.* Mineola, NY: Dover Publications, 1993.

Dalí, Salvador, and Haakon M. Chevalier. *50 Secrets of Magic Craftsmanship.* Mineola, NY: Dover Publications, 1992.

Dalí, Salvador, and J.G. Ballard. *Diary of a Genius.* Chicago, IL: Solar Books, 2007.

Grenier, Catherine. *Salvador Dalí: The Making of an Artist.* Paris, France: Flammarion, 2013.

King, Elliott H., and Montse Aguer Teixidor. *Salvador Dalí: The Late Work.* New Haven, CT: Yale University Press, 2010.

Shanes, Eric. *Salvador Dalí.* New York, NY: Parkstone Press, 2014.

Bibliography

Ades, Dawn. *Dalí*. New York, NY: Thames & Hudson, 1995.

Ades, Dawn, and Simon Baker, eds. *Undercover Surrealism, Georges Bataille and DOCUMENTS. Cambridge, MA:* MIT Press, 2006.

Aguer, Montserrat, and Fundación Gala-Salvador Dalí. *Salvador Dalí: An Illustrated Life.* London, England: Tate Publishing, 2007.

Brassaï, George. *Conversations with Picasso.* Chicago, IL: University of Chicago Press, 2003.

Caws, Mary Ann. *Salvador Dalí*. London, England Reaktion Books, 2008.

Dalí, Salvador. *Hidden Faces*. London, England: Peter Owen, 2007.

Dalí, Salvador. *The Secret Life of Salvador Dalí. Sussex, England* Alkin Books, 1993.

Elsohn, Ross. *Michael Salvador Dali and the Surrealists: Their Lives and Ideas*. Chicago, IL: Chicago Review Press, 2003.

Etherington-Smith, Meredith. *The Persistence of Memory: A Biography of Dalí*. New York, NY: Random House, 1993.

Fanés, Fèlix. *Salvador Dalí: The Construction of the Image, 1925–1930*. New Haven, CT: Yale University Press, 2007.

Finkelstein, Haim, ed. *The Collected Writings of Salvador Dalí*. New York, NY: Cambridge University Press, 1998.

Freud, Sigmund. *The Interpretation of Dreams.*New York, NY:Basic Books, 2010.

Gale, Matthew, ed. *Dalí and Film.* London, England: Tate Publishing, 2007.

Gibson, Ian. *The Shameful Life of Salvador Dalí.* London, England: Faber and Faber, 1998.

Hamalian, Linda. *The Cramoisy Queen: A Life of Caresse Crosby*. Carbondale, IL: Southern Illinois University Press, 2009.

Krauss, Rosalind. *The Optical Unconscious*. Cambridge, MA: MIT Press, 1996.

Lear, Amanda. *My Life with Dalí.* London, England: Virgin Books, 1985.

McGirk, Tim. *Wicked Lady: Salvador Dalí's Muse.* London, England: Headline, 1989.

Mundy, Jennifer, and Dawn Ades, eds. *Desire Unbound.* London, England Tate Publishing, 2001.

Raeburn, Michael, ed. *Salvador Dalí: The Early Years.* New York, NY: Thames & Hudson, 1994.

Rojas, Carlos. *Salvador Dalí: Or the Art of Spitting on Your Mother's Portrait*. University Park, PA: Pennsylvania State University Press, 1993.

Schaffner, Ingrid. *Salvador Dalí's Dream of Venus: The Surrealist Funhouse from the 1939 World's Fair.* Princeton, NJ: Princeton Architectural Press, 2002.

Index

T

V

W